I LIKE...

STARRING:

EEK! This book is missing SOMETHING!

In fact, it's missing A LOT OF THINGS.

Actually... it's kind of AMAZING that we printed it AT ALL, considering HOW MUCH WE LEFT OUT.

We're a little AFRAID to tell you JUST HOW MUCH of this book is missing because you're not SUPPOSED to publish a book that isn't finished,

BUT there's A LOT of stuff in here that we just didn't know the answers to. Because they're ALL ABOUT YOU!

So maybe you could help us out? You'll need a pen or a pencil or maybe some markers or crayons or glitter glue or a magazine and some scissors. And you'll need your brain and you'll definitely need your imagination.

AND

(This is the most important part of all)

you'll need YOU!

Because you're the ONLY one who really knows all about what you like and what you DON'T like —AND— who you ARE. ★

Whew. Thank you. You REALLY SAVED US. WE CAN'T WAIT to see what YOU have to SAY.

JUST A FEW FACTS

This is a picture of me:

My FAVORITE things to DO:

THESE ARE SOME things I DO NOT like to do:

Things I like to THINK ABOUT:

THESE ARE PEOPLE I Like:

Some things I LIKE ABOUT MYSELF:

So many things to Like!

Can you find EVERYTHING listed below? Why not **color** in your FAVORITES?

- A sloth in a beanie
- Tropical fruits
- A friendly robot
- Several birds (how many?)
- Three scoops of ice cream
- One dapper bow tie
- An athletic unicorn
- A cat having a daydream
- A happy NARWHAL
- An owl in boots
- A shy rabbit
- Someone in a top hat
- A place to go hiking
- A slightly soggy pizza party
- A motorcycle rider
- A creature in the tub
- Someone who likes the library

19

THE GALLERY OF ME

THIS FANTASTIC place is ALL ABOUT YOU. PEOPLE from all OVER the WORLD will come to VISIT just to learn WHO you ARE, WHAT you like, and what YOU'RE all about! These FRAMES + pedestals ARE READY to HOLD ALL the things YOU LIKE.

ARE you READY TO FILL THIS ROOM up to THE TOP? GO AHEAD! Ask an adult for some OLD MAGAZINES you can CUT up & START snipping out PICTURES OF THINGS you LIKE. GLUE them in RIGHT here! OR USE MARKERS, colored PENCILS, GLITTER glue, WHATEVER you need to CREATE YOUR VERY OWN WORLD-CLASS MUSEUM.

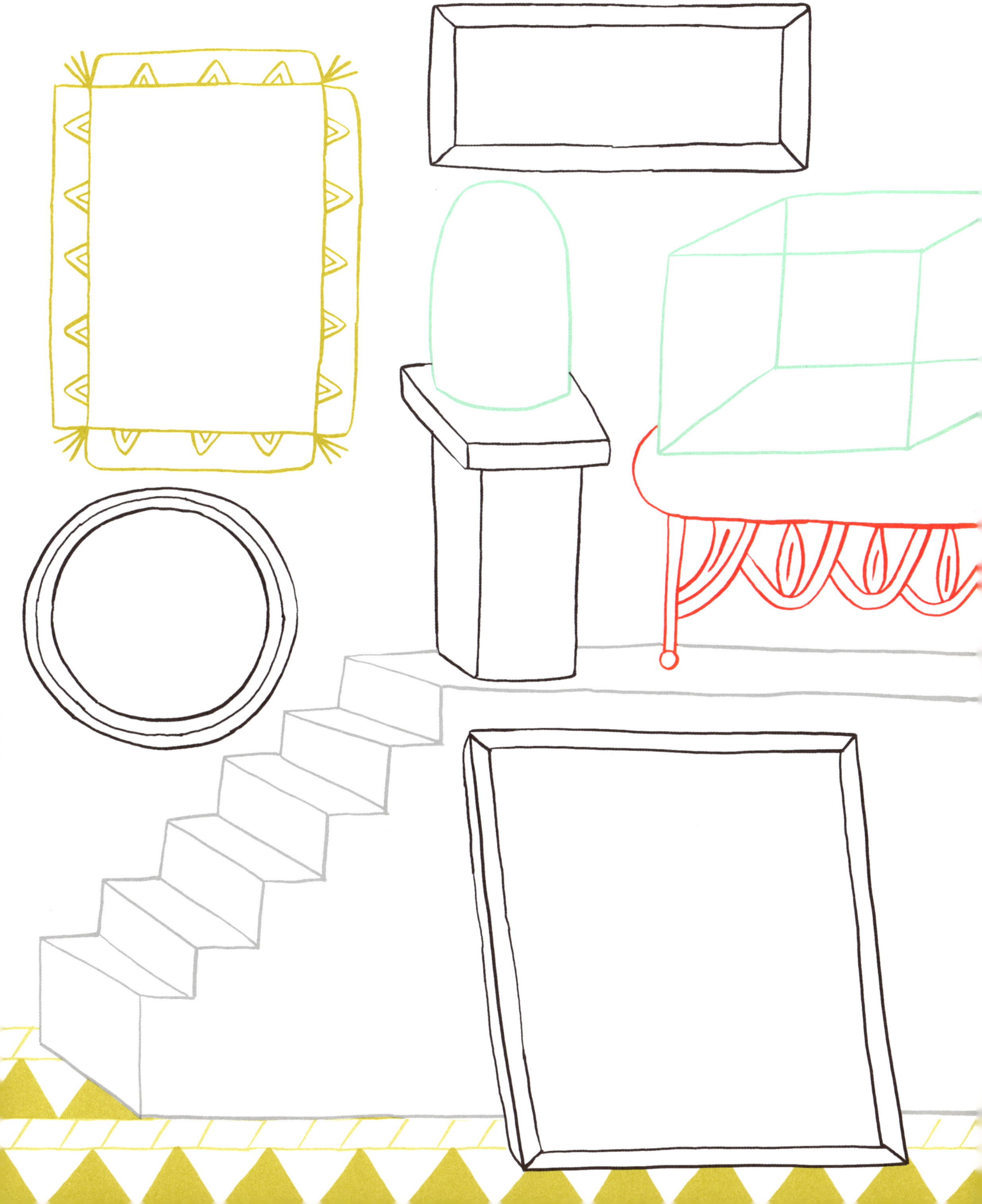

Congratulations!

You did it!

YOU REALLY DID IT!

You're officially the BEST person IN THE WORLD at something you really like to DO! (But you're going to have to tell us what it is...)

OFFICIALLY AWESOME

This CERTIFICATE of achievement is presented to _____
(NAME)

On this date _____ (TODAY'S DATE)

FOR being the BEST in the WORLD at _____ and _____!

And also for being REALLY, really GREAT at _____.

Oh, Goodness. There's an ANIMAL in YOUR BATHTUB. And it's filthy. But at least it's one you LIKE!

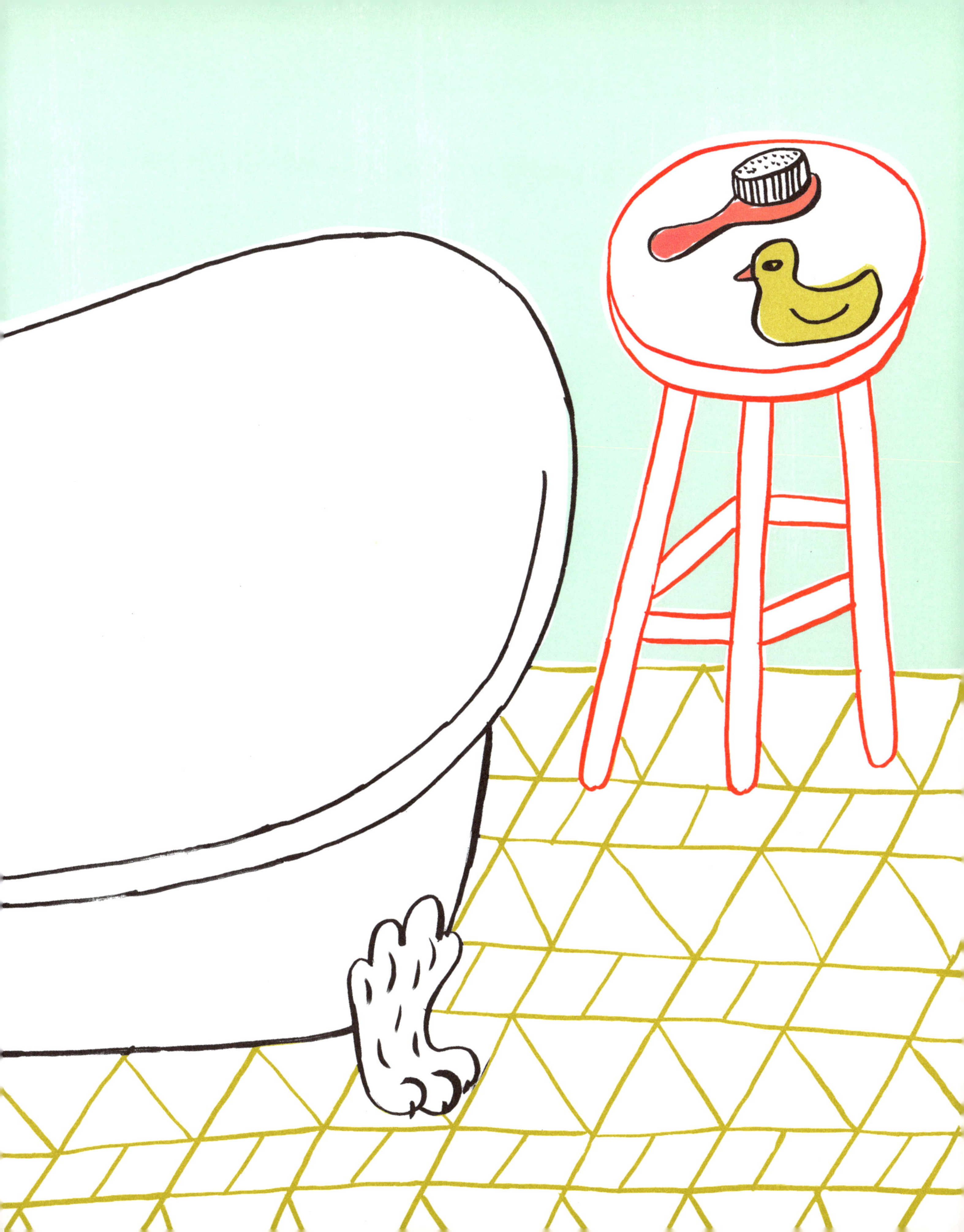

The leaders of the world have gotten together and agreed that you can have

YOUR VERY OWN HOLIDAY!

HOORAY!

...·...

EVERYONE AROUND HERE IS VERY EXCITED TO **CELEBRATE**

SO PLEASE tell US ALL ABOUT YOUR HOLIDAY SO WE CAN JOIN YOU! *

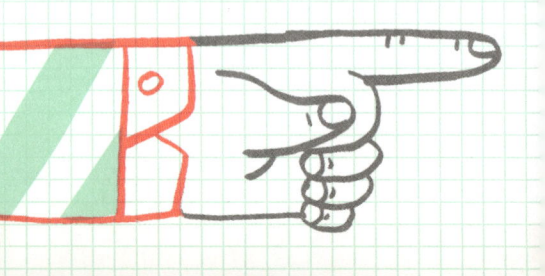

THE NAME OF MY HOLIDAY IS:

IT IS CELEBRATED ON THIS DATE:

THE REASON IT WAS INVENTED IS:

PEOPLE CELEBRATE BY WEARING:

AND SINGING THESE SONGS:

HERE ARE SOME ACTIVITIES WE DO ON THIS DAY:

AND THE FOODS WE EAT:

AND MY FAVORITE PART OF THE DAY IS THAT EVERYONE absolutely HAS to:

What are the COLORS YOU LIKE BEST?
* * *
Do you have lots of them? Or just a few?

Wouldn't it BE GREAT if instead of the USUAL color names, you got to name your OWN? You could choose silly names like YUCKY YELLOW or beautiful names like STRAWBERRY PIE or nice names LIKE CAT'S-EYE GREEN OR surprising names LIKE BIG TOENAIL. (EW! Big Toenail? GROSS! What kind of color is that?)

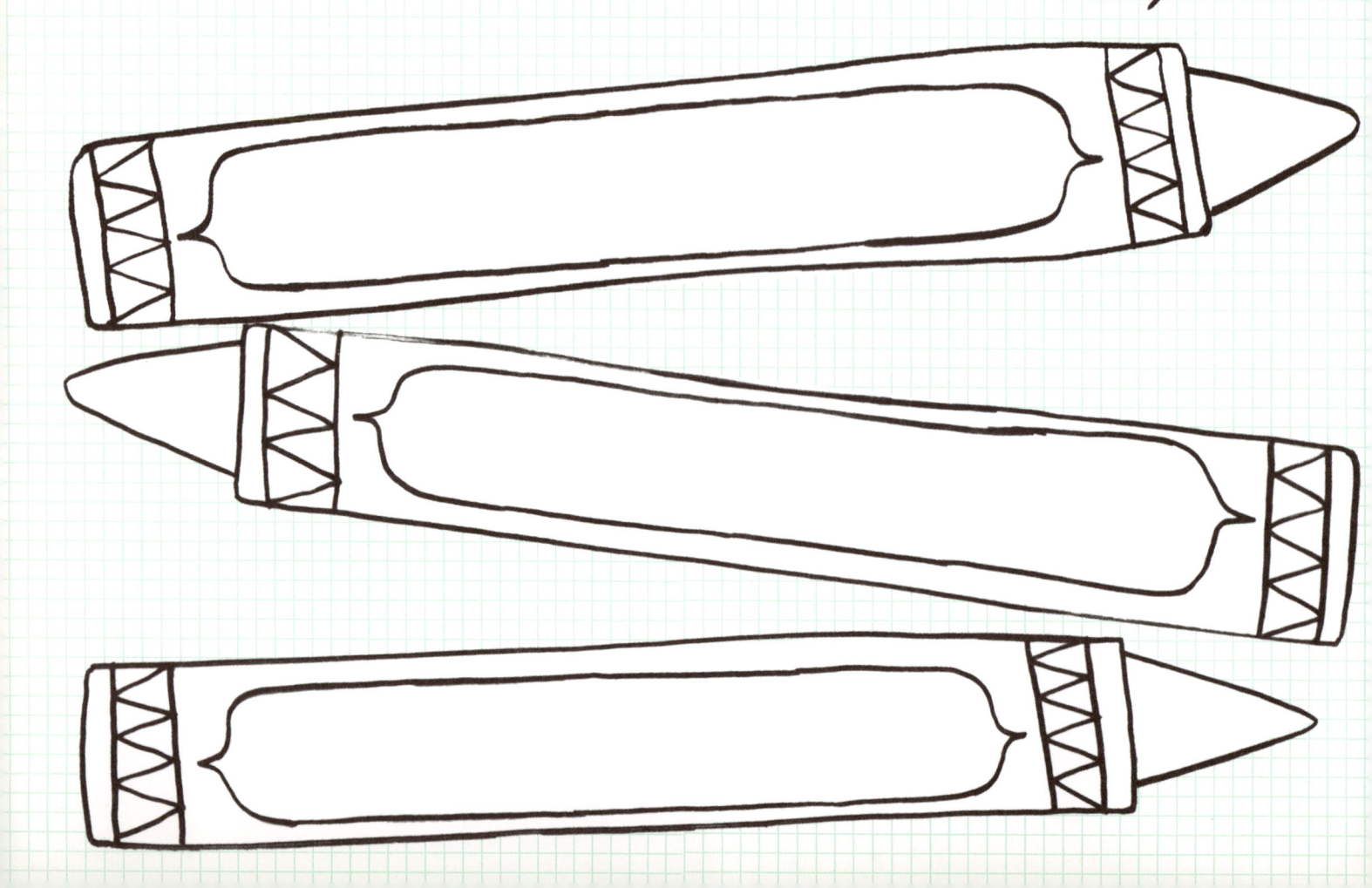

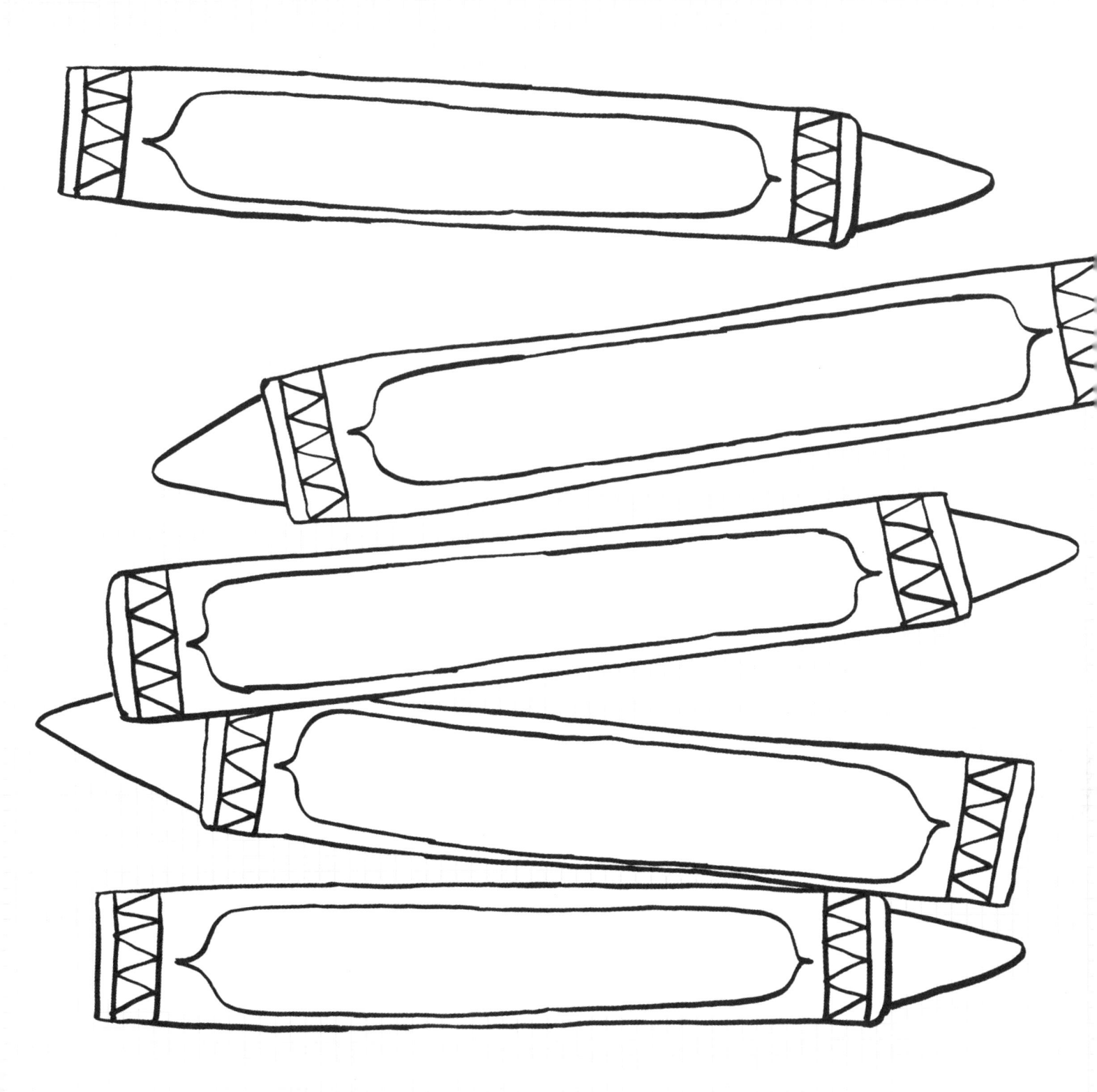

Well, anyway... THESE CRAYONS ARE JUST WAITING FOR YOU TO NAME them. SO color them IN, then LABEL THEM with a NEW NAME. A name that only YOU would ever CHOOSE. A name that is JUST RIGHT.

LET'S IMAGINE that TOMORROW is GOING TO BE A PERFECT DAY.

ah. That sounds nice.

And on a truly, REALLY, COMPLETELY PERFECT DAY, you get to do ALL the things you LIKE TO DO, and you don't have to do any OF the THINGS YOU don't LIKE TO DO.

So here's what you do right when you wake up:

Here's what you have for breakfast:

These people are with you:

Then you will go to:

And here's what you will do while you are there:

After that, you just might decide to:

And then, of course, you will stop here:

Everyone's getting a little tired. What's the grand finale before we all go home?

THIS IS A GIANT PIZZA! WE MADE IT JUST FOR YOU!

(THE ONLY PROBLEM IS, WE DIDN'T KNOW WHAT YOUR FAVORITE TOPPINGS ARE.) SOMEONE SUGGESTED peanut butter and GRAPES. someone else said you liked CELERY, BLUE cheese, and chocolate SAUCE. ALL TOGETHER? that sounded WEIRD tO US, SO WE THOUGHT We should LEAVE IT UP TO YOU.

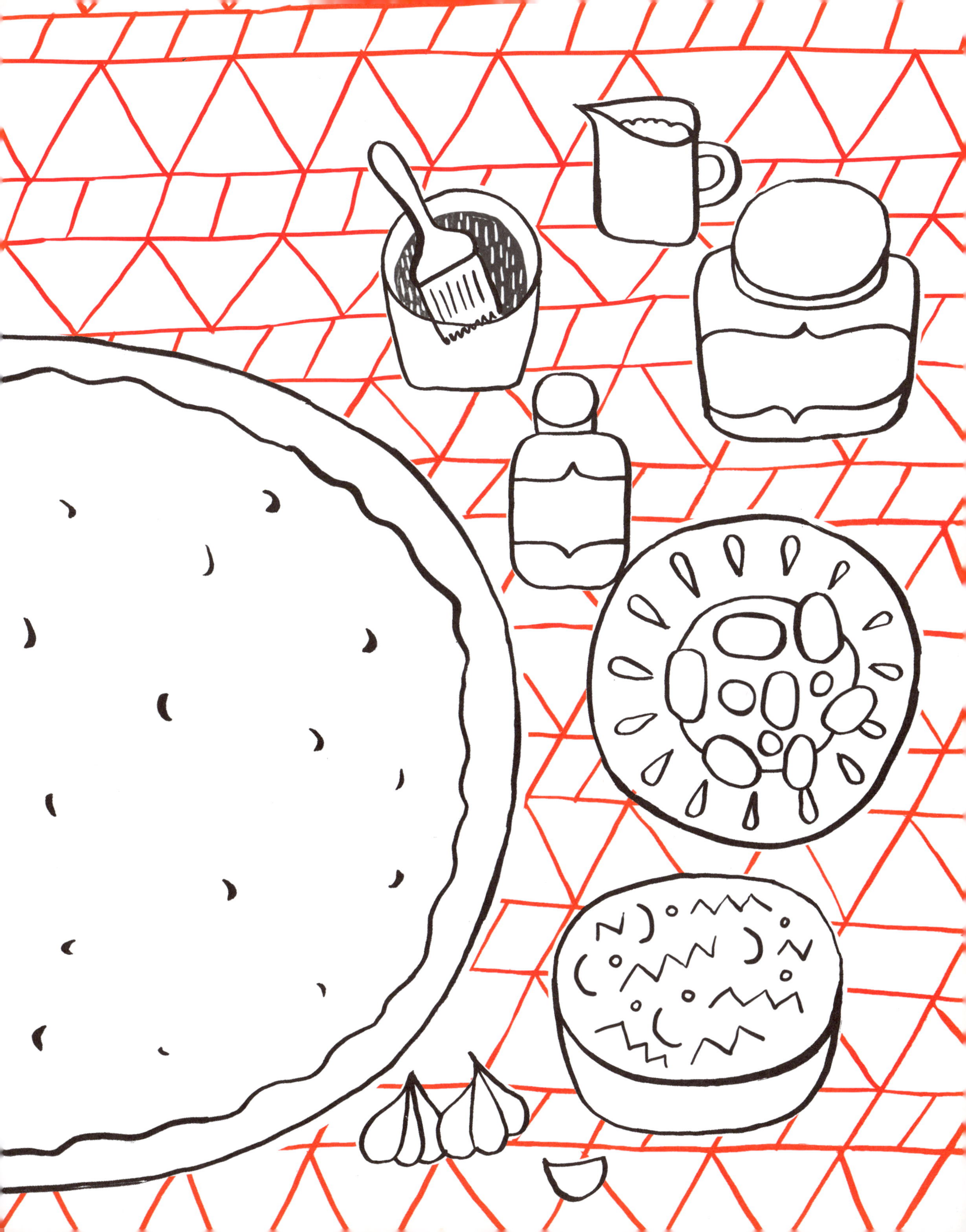

HAVE YOU EVER TAKEN A **SURVEY?** IT'S A GREAT WAY TO FIND THINGS OUT. AND YOU CAN **INTERVIEW** ANYONE YOU KNOW!

INSTRUCTIONS: WRITE THE NAMES OF PEOPLE YOU SURVEY ACROSS THE TOP, AND WRITE THEIR ANSWER (A OR B) IN EACH BOX. ONCE YOU'RE FINISHED, YOU CAN COMPARE YOUR ANSWERS. WHICH ONES ARE MOST POPULAR? ARE YOU SURPRISED BY ANYONE'S ANSWERS? WERE ANYONE'S ANSWERS EXACTLY THE SAME AS YOURS? OR COMPLETELY DIFFERENT?

NAME 1 | NAME 2 | NAME 3 | NAME 4

DO YOU PREFER (A) LAVENDER OR (B) TAN?

WOULD YOU RATHER BE (A) A HORSE OR (B) A RABBIT?

WOULD YOU RATHER HAVE (A) A PICKLE & PEANUT BUTTER SANDWICH OR (B) A CUP OF TOMATO AND GRAPEFRUIT SOUP?

Would you rather get around by (A) giraffe or (B) jet-powered skateboard?

Would you like to visit (A) 100 years into the future or (B) 100 years into the past?

Which would you like to visit: (A) the moon or (B) Japan?

Would you rather have (A) spaghetti for hair or (B) a strawberry for a nose?

Would you rather live (A) on a sailboat or (B) in a lighthouse?

Would you rather have (A) vanilla cake with chocolate frosting or (B) chocolate cake with vanilla frosting?

Would you rather be (A) a scientist or (B) a sculptor?

IMAGINE writing A LETTER to ALL the PEOPLE YOU like. Just to tell them you LIKE THEM. And to tell them WHY. Imagine how good those people will FEEL — to know that they ARE LIKED by someone. And that that SOMEONE is YOU!

It's EASY! You can photocopy the letter to the RIGHT, fill in YOUR ANSWERS, and send TO ANYONE YOU choose. HOW many PEOPLE do you want to send this letter to? WELL, THAT'S UP TO YOU.

hmph

date _____

Dear _____,

I just wanted to tell you I like you.
I like how _____ you are.
And how good you are at _____.
I like the way you _____.
And we always have fun when
we _____ together.

Thanks for being YOU!

From,
_____

If you could design any CREATURE you like, how would it look? What would YOU CALL IT? Would you want to keep it as a pet?

CIRCLE ALL the things your creature has, then DRAW it! Don't FORGET to draw it some food so it doesn't GET TOO HUNGRY...

We want your CREATURE to live for a LONG, LONG TIME.

- speckles
- LOTS of EYES
- FINS
- HORNS
- STRIPES
- Fangs
- SPOTS
- SCALES
- SPLOTCHES
- FUR
- GLOWS in the DARK
- A FEATHERY tail
- A SPIKY TAIL
- A LONG TAIL
- A SHORT tail
- wings

My ANIMAL lives in _____,
and LIKES TO EAT _____.
Any SPECIAL abilities? _____,
_____, _____.

What's on the Menu?

ICE CREAM!

But these are FLAVORS the world has NEVER seen.

Please COLOR them in and label them BECAUSE everyone around here is getting VERY HUNGRY!

Ran Bow ice cream

chrry partay

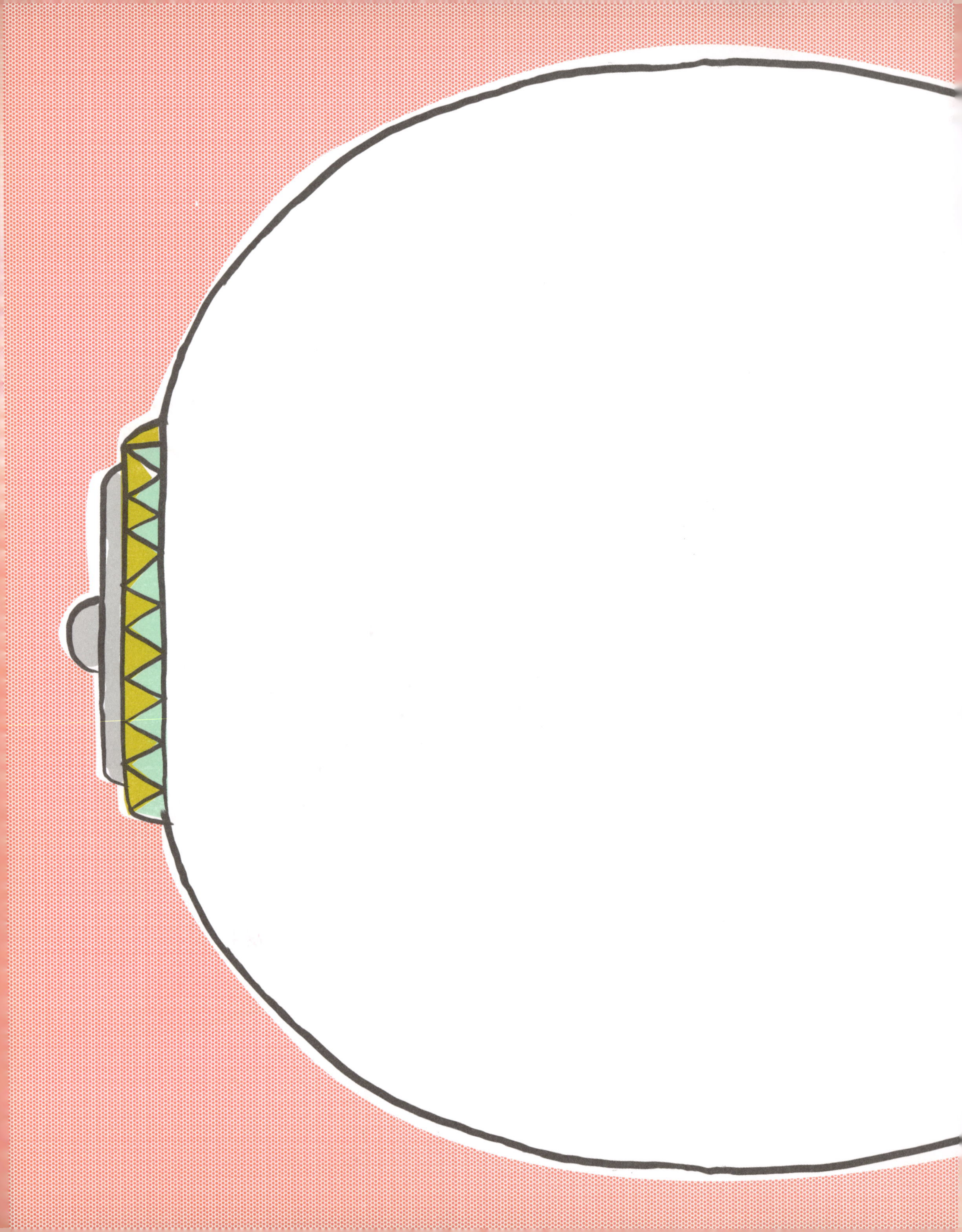

Would you fill it up? You can draw or paint or cut pictures out of a magazine (JUST ASK FIRST). GO ON... We're waiting with our quarters!

What a wonderful machine! You're pretty darn guaranteed for 25 cents, comb something AMAZING to get the only problem is it's empty right now!

This isn't just ANY ALPHABET.

This is an Alphabet of **THINGS YOU LIKE**, Things you *LOVE*, THINGS YOU ARE CRAZY ABOUT!

Here ARE 26 THINGS, from A to Z, that make YOU HAPPY. HOW will you start? APPLES? ANACONDAS? antelopes? ARTICHOKE HEARTS?

A   B

C   D   E   F

G   H   I   J

K L M N

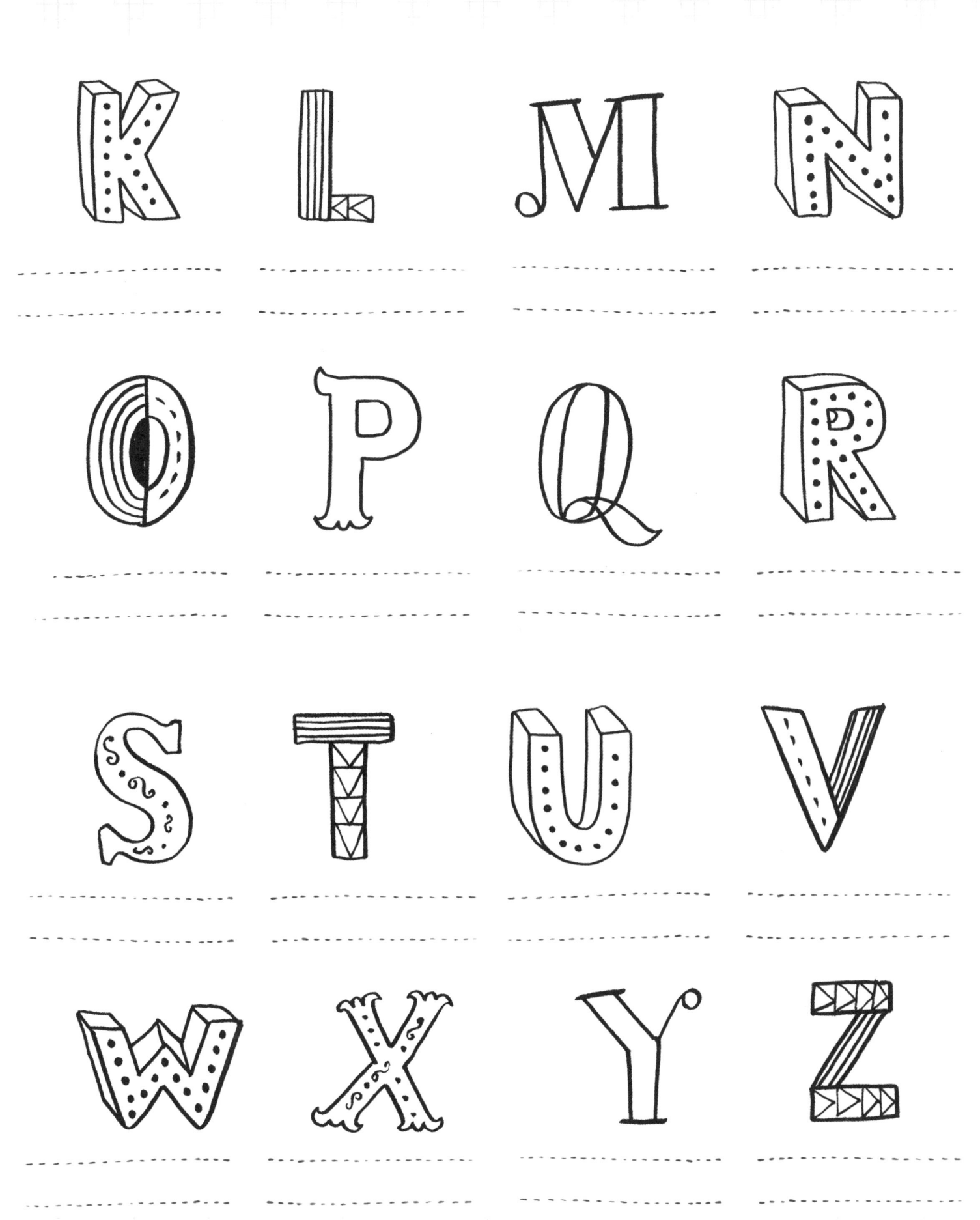

O P Q R

S T U V

W X Y Z

Which one would you LIKE?

CIRCLE A OR B, BUT ONLY ONE PER QUESTION!

A. A pet SHARK.
B. A PET Whale.

A. A toaster that PUTS A picture of YOUR FACE ON EVERY SLICE of toast.
B. A DOG that BARKS YOUR NAME.

A. A treehouse WITH A LIBRARY, a ROPE SWING, and a ZIP LINE.
B. AN IGLOO WITH A telescope, A STAINED glass WINDOW, and a HOT CHOCOLATE FOUNTAIN.

A. To BE the MAYOR OF A CITY OF SKY-SCRAPERS BUILT in OUTER SPACE.
B. To BE THE RULER of an underWATER WORLD built ENTIRELY of GLASS BUBBLES.

A. The world's largest collection of socks that have lost their match.

B. The world's largest collection of stickers that are no longer sticky.

A. The ability to read people's minds.

B. The ability to predict the future.

A. You can't walk normally— you always have to skip.

B. You can't speak normally— you always have to sing.

A. A constellation named after you.

B. A species of jungle animal named after you.

SPECIAL EDITION

EXTRA GOOD NEWS
EXTRA GOOD NEWS

IN YOUR FAMILY:

_____
_____
_____
_____
_____

This newspaper is filled with things you want to hear

Something that's happening in the world:

_____
_____
_____
_____
_____

GOOD NEWS ABOUT YOU:

AND WHO'S in the PICTURES ON THE FRONT PAGE?

AT YOUR SCHOOL:

WHAT MADE THE HEADLINES THIS WEEK?

WHAT DOES YOUR FUTURE HOLD?

Do you think that in the future you will like the same things? What will you look like? What will you wear? How will you style your future hair???

Dear FUTURE _____ (NAME),

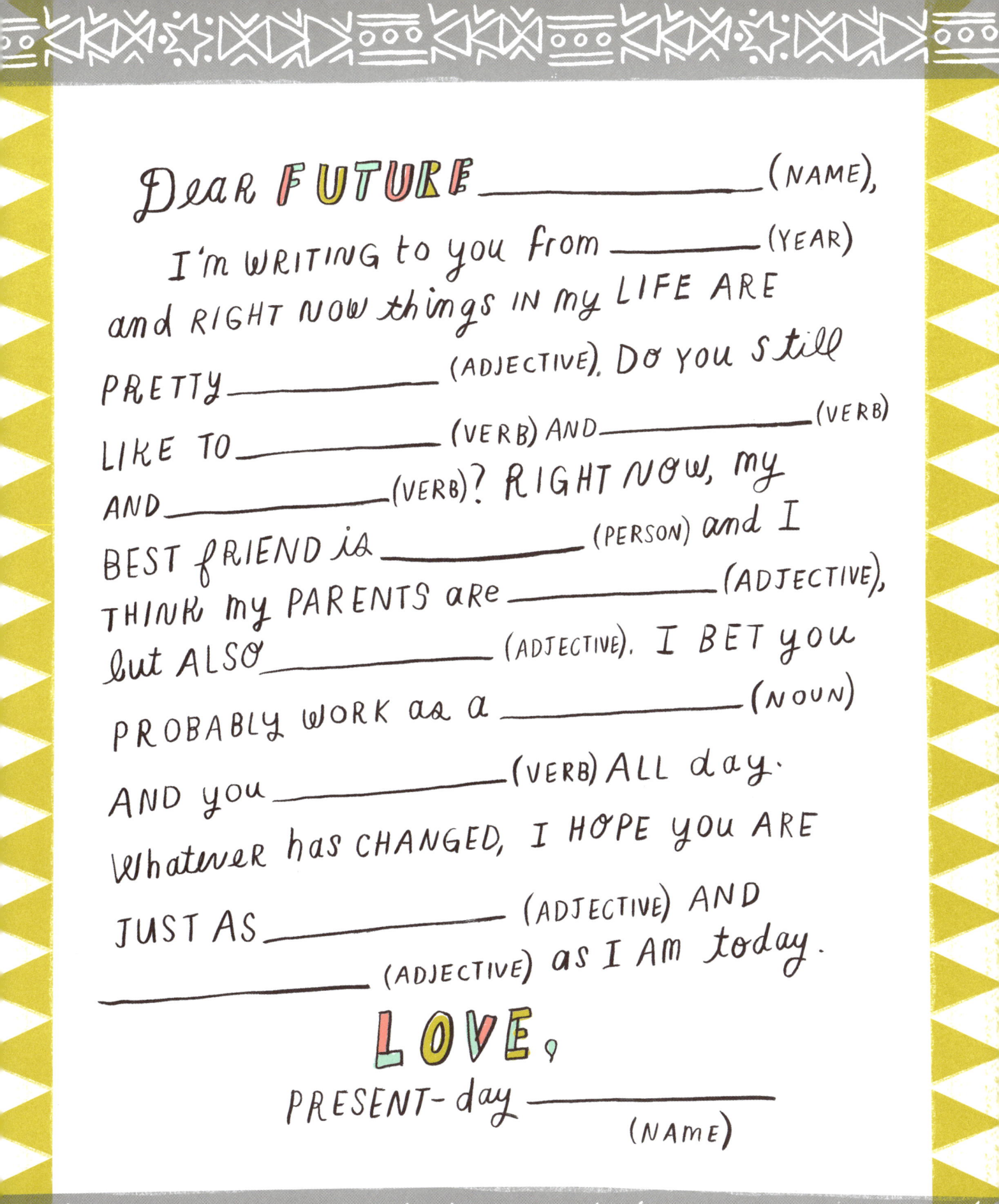

I'm writing to you from _____ (YEAR) and right now things in my LIFE ARE PRETTY _____ (ADJECTIVE). Do you still LIKE TO _____ (VERB) AND _____ (VERB) AND _____ (VERB)? RIGHT NOW, my BEST FRIEND is _____ (PERSON) and I THINK my PARENTS are _____ (ADJECTIVE), but ALSO _____ (ADJECTIVE). I BET you PROBABLY WORK as a _____ (NOUN) AND you _____ (VERB) ALL day. Whatever has CHANGED, I HOPE YOU ARE JUST AS _____ (ADJECTIVE) AND _____ (ADJECTIVE) as I AM today.

LOVE,

PRESENT-day _____ (NAME)

COMPENDIUM
live inspired

Written by: M.H. CLARK
WHO ESPECIALLY LIKES THE SMELL OF OLD BOOKS

Illustrated & designed by: SARAH WALSH
WHO HAS A SERIOUS WEAKNESS FOR CINNAMON ROLLS

Edited by: AMELIA RIEDLER & KRISTIN EADE

Creative Direction by: JULIE FLAHIFF & HEIDI DYER

With SPECIAL THANKS to the ENTIRE COMPENDIUM FAMILY.

ISBN: 978-1-938298-81-3

© 2015 by Compendium, Inc. All rights reserved. No part of this publication may be reproduced or transmitted in any form or by any means, electronic or mechanical, including photocopy, recording, or any storage and retrieval system now known or to be invented without written permission from the publisher. Contact: Compendium, Inc., 2100 North Pacific Street, Seattle, WA 98103. *I Like…*; Compendium; live inspired; and the format, design, layout, and coloring used in this book are trademarks and/or trade dress of Compendium, Inc. This book may be ordered directly from the publisher, but please try your local bookstore first. Call us at 800.91.IDEAS, or come see our full line of inspiring products at live-inspired.com

1st printing. Printed in China with soy inks. A011511001